I Can Read

by Michèle Dufresne

PIONEER VALLEY EDUCATIONAL PRESS, INC.

I can read to my mom.

Jack and Jenny Jack
A PLAYMATE FOR JACK

I can read to my dad.

I can read to my sister.

I can read to my brother.

I can read to my grandpa.

11

I can read to my grandma.

I can read to my friend.

I can read to myself.